The Little

By
Muon Van

Illustrated by
JoAnn Adinolfi

Creston Books

In the shadows of an old forest
stood a little tree.
She was so small,
she was the smallest tree of all.

When the little tree was a young sapling,
the forest ranged farther than the eye could see.

Now, after many seasons of less and less rain,
the little tree could easily tell where the forest
began and where it ended.

The new trees were smaller, too.
The older trees had grown so tall,
they had almost touched the stars.
The new trees could barely see over
their ancestors' knees.

The littlest tree of all worried.
The little tree looked at her little seed.

The sun rose and the
sun set.

The little tree looked up
at the stars and wondered,

"What do they see?"

One day, a brown bird flew by.
The little tree asked the brown
bird, "Have you traveled far?"
"Yes," the bird answered.
"I have flown very far."

The little tree asked the brown bird,
"Are trees this small everywhere?"
"Not at all," the bird said. "I have seen a place
  where trees grow a hundred feet tall!"

The little tree asked the brown bird,
"Are trees this bare everywhere?"
"No," the bird answered. "I have seen a place
  where the leaves are so thick, you can sit
  in the shade all day!"

The little tree was quiet.

Then she asked the brown bird, "Are there trees like me there?" "Yes," the bird said. "There are trees like you there. There are trees with ruffly heads and trees with long noses. There are trees with pointy ears and trees with stubby toes. Trees from all over the world grow there."

"Thank you," said the little tree
to the brown bird.
Then she closed her eyes and
hugged her little seed.

The sun rose and the sun set.
When the little tree saw the brown bird again,
she asked him, "Will you do a favor for me?
Will you flap your wings with all your might?"
The bird agreed.

The little tree cradled her little seed.
The brown bird flapped his wings with
all his might.
And the little tree let go of her little seed.

"Goodbye, little seed," said the little tree.
But the little seed was already gone.

The little seed floated.
The little seed dipped.

The little seed danced
in the breeze.

The little seed sailed over the crowns of trees.

The little seed flew so high,

it nearly touched the stars.

The sun rose and the sun set.
The little tree lost count of the seasons.
The forest was smaller than ever.
And the little tree was no longer the littlest tree
of all, though she was no bigger than before.
The little tree thought often of her little seed.

The sun rose and the sun set.
Finally, the brown bird flew back again.
The little tree asked the brown bird,
"Where is my little seed? Is it strong
and tall? Does it remember me at all?"
But this time, the brown bird had
no answers.

The sun rose and the sun set.
The brown bird came again to the little tree.
This time, before the little tree asked anything,
the bird said, "I've heard of a very special tree.
It is so tall, its shadow covers the biggest mountain.
It is so strong, a hundred elephants cannot knock it down.
And it has leaves so bright, they blind the sun.
I will ask this tree if it has seen your little seed."

Again the sun rose and the sun set.
The brown bird returned.
The brown bird said to the little tree,
"The tallest, strongest, brightest tree
is sending its answer soon."

And there in the breeze floated a leaf.

The leaf was the color of emeralds.
The leaf was as big as the moon.
The leaf twirled and shimmered.
It flew so high, it nearly touched the stars.

The leaf floated down.

Until it landed.

And the little tree knew.
"My little seed," said the little tree.
"You're not so little anymore!
You're taller than the tallest mountain
and stronger than the strongest elephant.
You're brighter than the sun

and still you remember me!"

Author's Note

The Little Tree was written for my mother, who is both the little tree and the little seed.

After the Vietnamese-American war, my maternal grandfather and his children planned to escape the oppressive post-war Vietnamese regime. By secretly accumulating food and gasoline rations, my mother and her brothers saved enough resources for a long-distance boat trip out of Vietnamese waters.

Though he supplied the boat, my grandfather refused to flee with his children. He could not abandon care of the ancestral altar, even if it meant never seeing his children again.

My mother, her brothers, and their families survived the perilous East Asian waters and landed in a Hong Kong refugee camp. After a year in the camp, they were flown east to their new homes in the United States.

Like other women from her village who had fled as part of the "boat people" exodus, my mother did not speak English, did not drive, and did not work outside of the home. This was a stark contrast to the life she lived in Vietnam, where she had been completely autonomous and, at one point during the war, raised two children single-handedly.

In America, my mother gave birth to five more sons, for a total of nine children. Though she did not send her children geographically elsewhere, she sent them educationally and culturally elsewhere. She had completed only the third grade but all her children went to college and some attained Master's degrees. Most of them preferred to speak English at home. They laughed at jokes and argued about things she couldn't understand. She couldn't even understand what some of them did for work and couldn't explain it to those who asked.

So my mother, once the little seed, had become the little tree. The physical circumstances were different but the emotional ones were just as daunting as those her father faced. She must have wondered: Am I brave enough for the job? Have I done everything I can? When the time comes, will I be able to let my child go so she can live a life I can't even imagine?

These questions are part of every parent's journey, and for an immigrant parent, the questions can be especially poignant. *The Little Tree* will resonate with both parents and children as they explore what it means to love and be loved in this story about a brave, little tree and her precious, only seed.

Muon Van lives in the hills of Northern California, where there are trees with graceful branches and trees with bashful leaves. There are trees with fickle bark and trees with stubborn roots. Trees, and people, from all over the world live and grow there. Her previous title with Creston Books, *In a Village by the Sea,* received starred reviews from Kirkus and Publishers Weekly.

JoAnn Adinolfi is the illustrator of many books for young readers. She happily grew up on Staten Island in New York surrounded by a big, Italian family and lots of trees. Now she happily lives in New Hampshire with her husband and enjoys digging holes to plant trees which she likes to watch grow along with her two children. Visit her at joannadinolfi.com.